Items should be returned on or before the last date shown below. Items not already requested by other borrowers may be renewed in person, in writing or by telephone. To renew, please quote the number on the barcode label. To renew online a PIN is required. This can be requested at your local library.
Renew online @ **www.dublincitypubliclibraries.ie**
Fines charged for overdue items will include postage incurred in recovery. Damage to or loss of items will be charged to the borrower.

Leabharlanna Poiblí Chathair Bhaile Átha Cliath
Dublin City Public Libraries

Dublin City
Baile Átha Cliath

Brainse Mheal Ráthluirc
Charleville Mall Branch
Tel: 8749619

Date Due	Date Due	Date Due
13. JUN 12.		
NOV	17. SEP 15.	
08. AUG 13.	07. NOV 15	
29. APR 14.	19th March	
10. JUN 15.		
03. SEP 15.		

First published in 2006 by
Franklin Watts
338 Euston Road
London
NW1 3BH

Franklin Watts Australia
Hachette Children's Books
Level 17/207 Kent Street
Sydney
NSW 2000

A CIP catalogue record for this book is available
from the British Library.

ISBN 978 0 7496 6809 9

Series Editor: Jackie Hamley
Series Advisor: Dr Barrie Wade
Series Designer: Peter Scoulding

Printed in China

Franklin Watts is a division of
Hachette Children's Books
an Hachette UK company.
www.hachette.co.uk

Monster Cake

by Damian Harvey

Illustrated by Graham Philpot

W

FRANKLIN WATTS
LONDON•SYDNEY

There was once a baker
who baked a huge cake ...

... not just any old cake,

but a MONSTER cake!

He mixed it all up
in the big kitchen sink.

And the things that he used

made a terrible stink.

He dropped in four slugs ...

... some slime ...

... and a shoe.

Then in went five snails ...

... six spiders ...

... and goo.

He shovelled in muck ...

... and a sweaty old sock.

A slimy, dead fish ...

... and some big chunks
of rock.

He collected some cheese
of the smelliest sort.

Then added some beetles
and bugs that he'd caught.

He put it all into
the oven to bake.

25

And when it was ready,
he sliced up that cake.

The monsters
soon munched it,
and ate the plates, too.

But he saved one
last piece ...

... and that's just for you!

Leapfrog Rhyme Time has been specially designed to fit the requirements of the Literacy Framework. It offers real books for beginner readers by top authors and illustrators.

RHYME TIME

Mr Spotty's Potty
ISBN 978 0 7496 3831 3

Eight Enormous Elephants
ISBN 978 0 7496 4634 9

Freddie's Fears
ISBN 978 0 7496 4382 9

Squeaky Clean
ISBN 978 0 7496 6805 1

Craig's Crocodile
ISBN 978 0 7496 6806 8

Felicity Floss: Tooth Fairy
ISBN 978 0 7496 6807 5

Captain Cool
ISBN 978 0 7496 6808 2

Monster Cake
ISBN 978 0 7496 6809 9

The Super Trolley Ride
ISBN 978 0 7496 6810 5

The Royal Jumble Sale
ISBN 978 0 7496 6811 2

But, Mum!
ISBN 978 0 7496 6812 9

Dan's Gran's Goat
ISBN 978 0 7496 6814 3

Lighthouse Mouse
ISBN 978 0 7496 6815 0

Big Bad Bart
ISBN 978 0 7496 6816 7

Ron's Race
ISBN 978 0 7496 6817 4

Alfie the Sea Dog
ISBN 978 0 7496 7958 3

Red Riding Hood Rap
ISBN 978 0 7496 7959 0

Pets on Parade
ISBN 978 0 7496 7960 6

Let's Dance
ISBN 978 0 7496 7961 3

Benny and the Monster
ISBN 978 0 7496 7962 0

Bathtime Rap
ISBN 978 0 7496 7963 7

Boris the Spider
ISBN 978 0 7496 7791 6

Miss Polly's Seaside Brolly
ISBN 978 0 7496 7792 3

The Lonely Pirate
ISBN 978 0 7496 7793 0

Woolly the Bully
ISBN 978 0 7496 7098 6*
ISBN 978 0 7496 7790 9

Juggling Joe
ISBN 978 0 7496 7103 7*
ISBN 978 0 7496 7795 4

What a Frog!
ISBN 978 0 7496 7102 0*
ISBN 978 0 7496 7794 7

I Wish!
ISBN 978 0 7496 7940 8*
ISBN 978 0 7496 7952 1

Raindrop Bill
ISBN 978 0 7496 7941 5*
ISBN 978 0 7496 7953 8

Sir Otto
ISBN 978 0 7496 7942 2*
ISBN 978 0 7496 7954 5

Queen Rosie
ISBN 978 0 7496 7943 9*
ISBN 978 0 7496 7955 2

Giraffe's Good Game
ISBN 978 0 7496 7944 6*
ISBN 978 0 7496 7956 9

Miss Lupin's Motorbike
ISBN 978 0 7496 7945 3*
ISBN 978 0 7496 7957 6

Other Leapfrog titles also available:

Leapfrog Fairy Tales

A selection of favourite fairy tales, simply retold.

Leapfrog

Fun, original stories by top authors and illustrators.

Leapfrog World Tales

Fun retellings of stories from around the world.

For more details, go to:

www.franklinwatts.co.uk

* hardback